Written by Jill Eggleton
Illustrated by Paul Könye

Tilly had a sheep farm with two hundred woolly sheep. The sheep all looked the same and they all did the same things. If one sheep went into the mud, they all went into the mud.

"Sheep are boring," said Tilly. "They just copy each other."

Ba-a-a-a!
Ba-a-a-a!
Ba-a-a-a!
Ba-a-a-a!
Ba-a-a-a!

Tilly had to watch her sheep every day. If one sheep went under the fence and onto the road, they all went under the fence and onto the road. If one sheep fell in a hole, they all fell in a hole.

"Why do you copy each other?" asked Tilly. "Can't you think for yourselves?"

Ba-a-a-a!
Ba-a-a-a!
Ba-a-a-a!
Silly sheep!

But Tilly had so many sheep, she didn't notice Shamus. Shamus didn't copy the other sheep.

He didn't **ba-a-a-a** when they did, and he didn't go with them anywhere.

When Tilly came to get the sheep for shearing, Shamus hid in a rock cave.

Ba-a-a-a!
Ba-a-a-a!
Ba-a-a-a!
Ba-a-a-a!

All the sheep went into the pen, one after the other. When they came back, they all looked the same – skinny and bare, like chickens ready for cooking.

Shamus stayed in his rock cave and only came out to eat.

Tilly never counted her sheep, so she didn't know that one was missing.

Shamus' wool grew longer and longer.
It grew so long, that one day when he came out of his cave, he fell over.
His wool was so heavy, he couldn't get up.

The other sheep didn't know what he was.
They walked around and around him, one after the other, sniffing him with their wet noses.

Sniff-sniff
Sniff-sniff!
Ba-a-a-a!

But the sheep got tangled up in Shamus' long wool and they fell on top of him in a big heap. They made so much noise that Tilly came out.

"You silly sheep," said Tilly.
"Why do you have to copy each other?"
Then she saw Shamus.
"Yikes!" she said.
"You need your wool cut."

Ba-a-a-a!
Yikes!

Shamus couldn't walk, so Tilly had to get the tractor to carry him to the pen.

"You are not like the other sheep," she said. "You are like a woolly mammoth."

Tilly got the clippers. Then she put them down.

"I don't think you want to be like the other sheep," she said.

Now Tilly has a sheep farm with two hundred woolly sheep that all look the same.

All except for one.

One sheep has dreadlocks!

Ba-a-a-a!
Cool sheep!
Ba-a-a-a!

Headlines

Headlines can look different.

Headlines in a magazine

Guide Notes

Title: Shamus
Stage: Launching Fluency – Orange

Genre: Fiction
Approach: Guided Reading
Processes: Thinking Critically, Exploring Language, Processing Information
Written and Visual Focus: Newspaper Headlines, Speech Bubbles, Thought Bubble
Word count: 386

Thinking Critically

(sample questions)

- What do you think this story could be about? Look at the title and discuss.
- Look at the cover. Why do you think Tilly has her hands on her hips?
- Look at pages 2 and 3. Do you think Tilly was right to think the sheep were boring? Why do you think that?
- Look at pages 4 and 5. Why do you think the sheep copy each other?
- Look at pages 6 and 7. Why do you think Shamus didn't want to be shorn?
- Look at pages 10 and 11. Why do you think the sheep were sniffing Shamus?
- Look at pages 14 and 15. What do you think made Tilly change her mind about clipping Shamus?

Exploring Language

Terminology

Author and illustrator credits, ISBN number

Vocabulary

Clarify: dreadlocks, woolly, shearing, pen
Singular/Plural: thing/things, chicken/chickens, nose/noses, sheep/sheep
Homonyms: road/rode, hole/whole, bare/bear

Print Conventions

Apostrophes – contraction (can't, didn't, couldn't, don't), possessive (Shamus'); dash

Phonological Patterns

Focus on short and long vowels **e** (sh**ee**p, f**e**ll, g**e**t, **e**ach, w**e**nt)
Discuss endings and root words (tripp**ed**, sniff**ing**, miss**ing**)